Mark Evans

SCARLET HOOD

Illustrated by
Isobel Lundie

SCRIBO

Published in Great Britain in MMXVIII by
Scribo, an imprint of
The Salariya Book Company Ltd
25 Marlborough Place, Brighton BN1 1UB
www.salariya.com

ISBN: 978-1-912233-34-2

SALARIYA

SCRIBO BOOK HOUSE SCRIBBLERS

Text copyright © Mark Evans MMXVIII

1 3 5 7 9 8 6 4 2

A CIP catalogue record for this book is available
from the British Library.

Printed and bound in China.
Printed on paper from sustainable sources.

Visit
www.salariya.com
for our online catalogue and
free fun stuff.

PAPER FROM

SUSTAINABLE
FORESTS

Author: Mark Evans studied
Theatre and Film at Curtin University.
He has been a professional actor and
drama teacher for over 20 years,
appearing on film, TV and stage in
Australia. He is now an exciting new
writer for children who specialises in
adventure and fantasy fiction.

Artist: Isobel Lundie graduated
from Kingston University in 2015
where she studied Illustration and
Animation. She has always been
interested in how to make books
interactive so children can lose
themselves in the narrative and escape
to another world.

SCARLET HOOD

At the top of the world

on a white winter shore,

Scarlet arrives in Norway.

Her 'itchy feet' family   move around a lot,   so new faces

and places

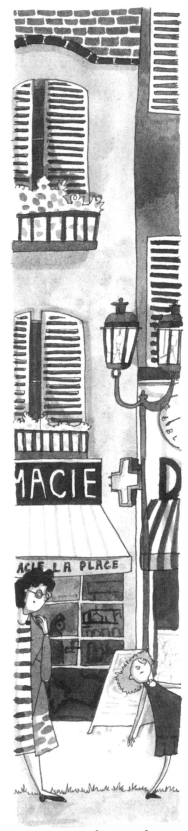

are normal to Scarlet.

London,

Shanghai,   Sao Paulo,   Budapest,

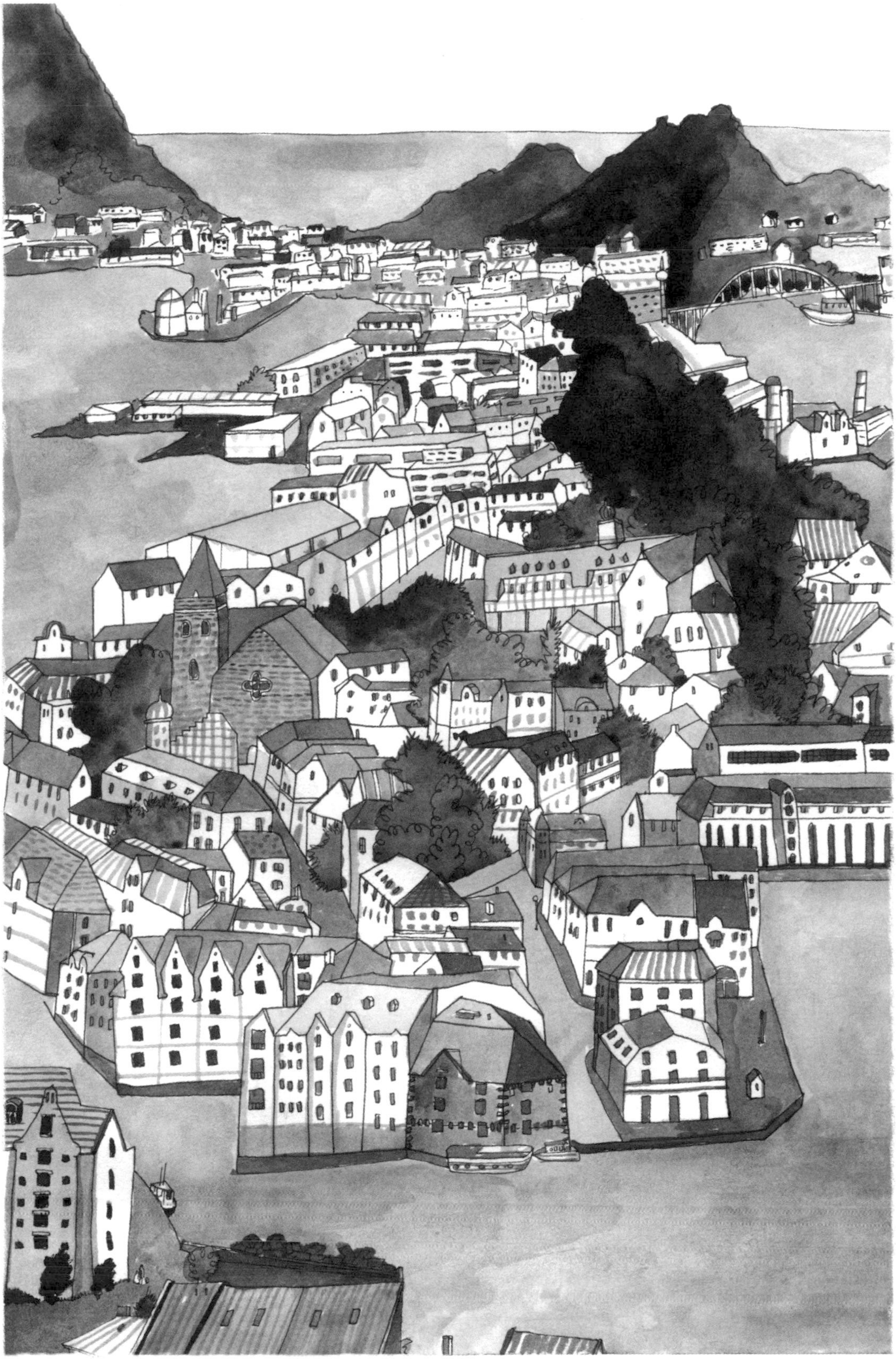

and now Norway.

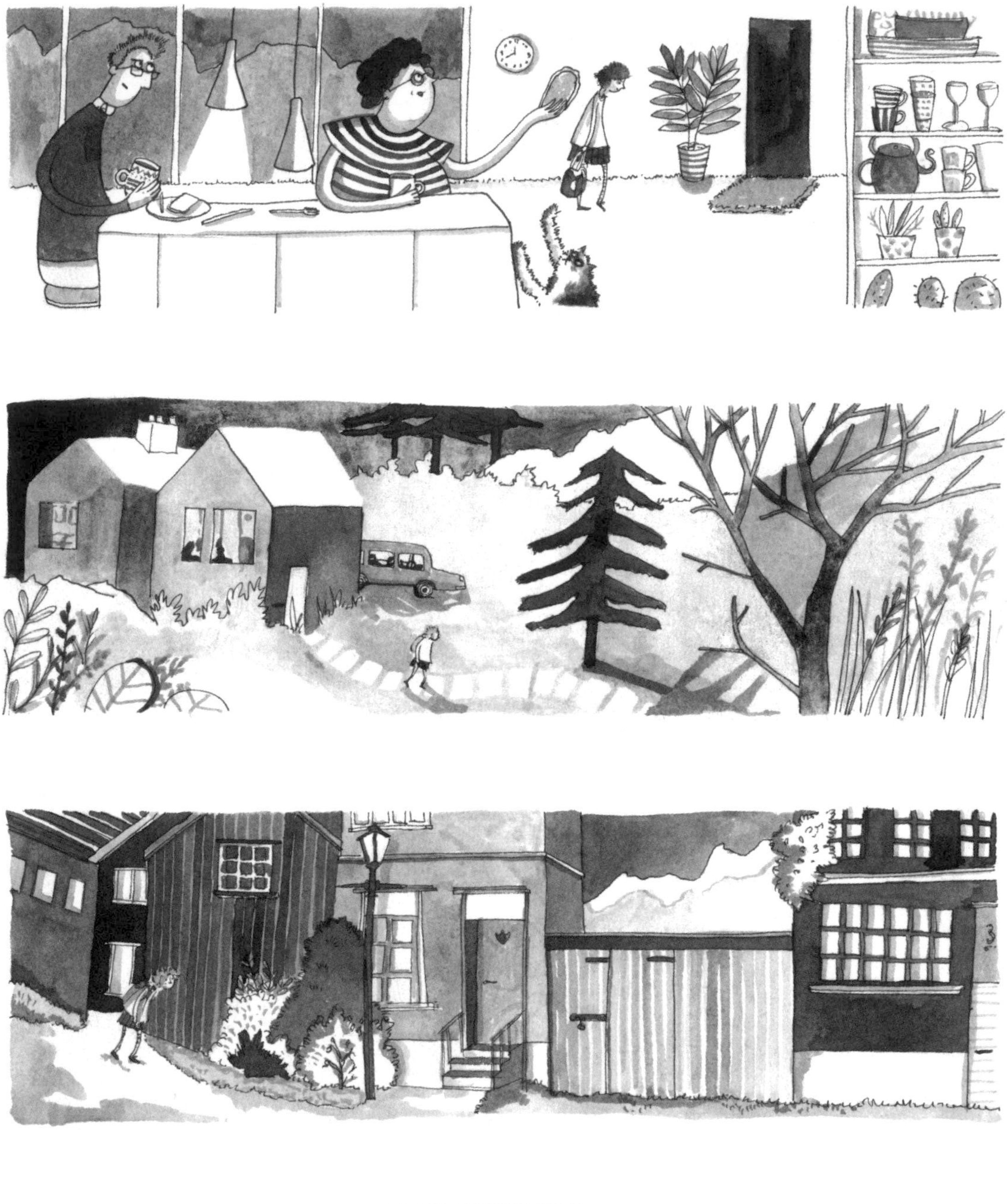

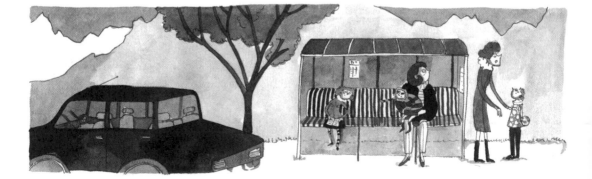

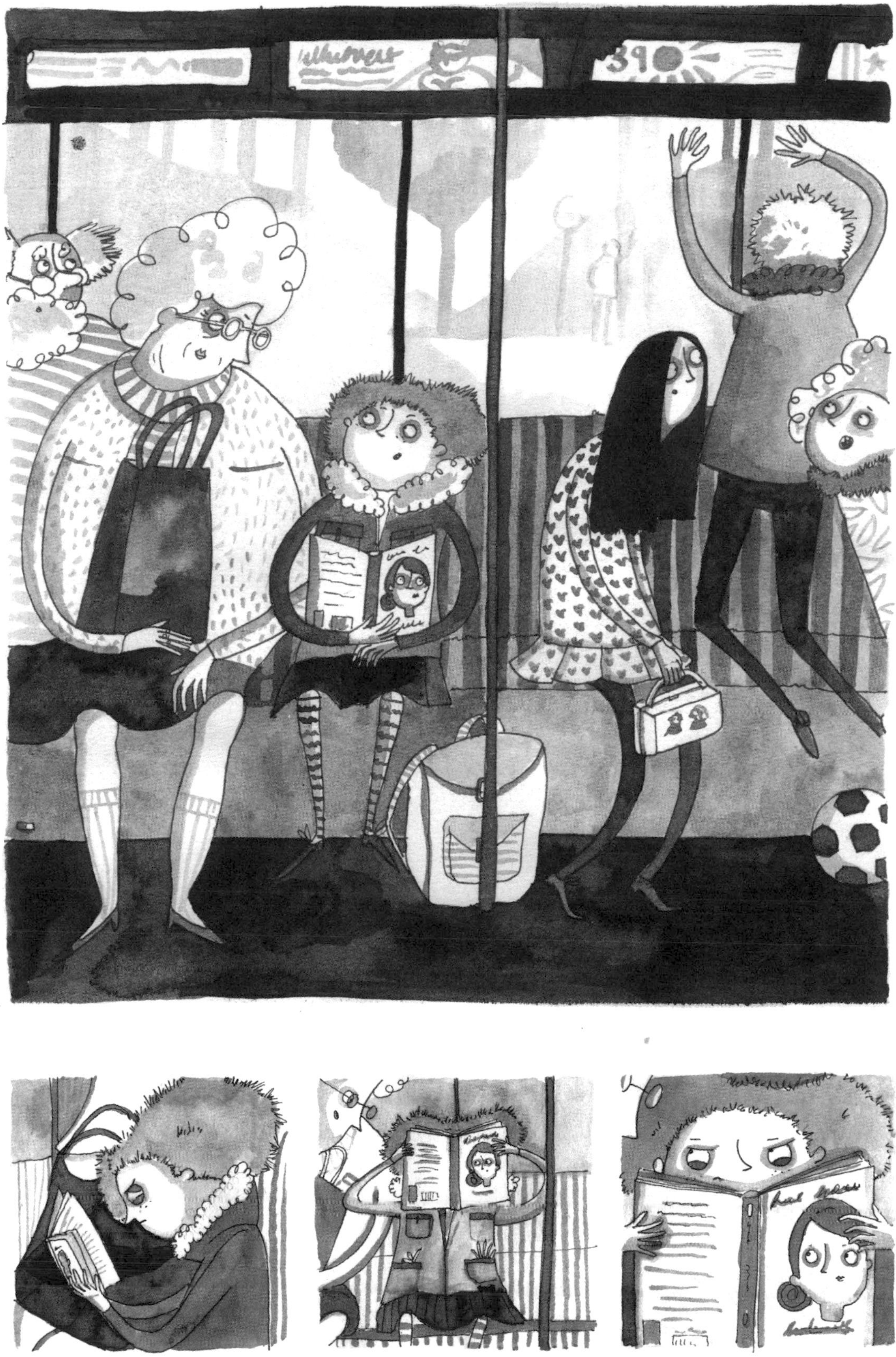

Sofie Sande

Marcus Kolden

Ivan Haestad

Henry Femrite

Ellen Arvesen

Lina Egeland

Mr Fugleberg

Annie Bingen

Evelyn Holten

Jonas Borresen

Dan Fiske

But all is not well at her new school

because in the playground Scarlet must face a bully.

The children all call this bully Greta the Cruel.

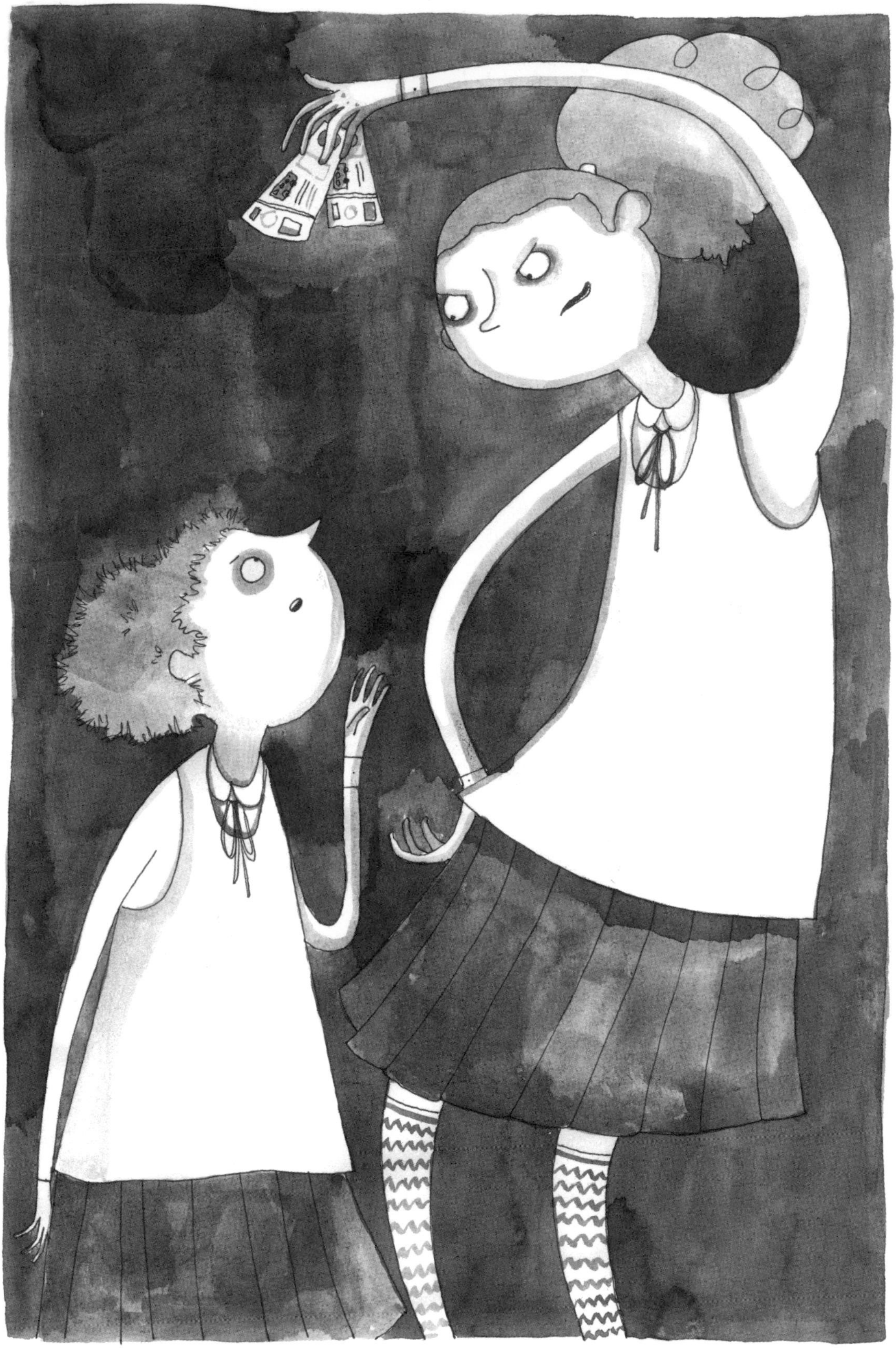

She is a giant.

She is menacing.

She is mean.

Every day is the same:

Greta taunts

and teases

and calls her names

and dips her hair in ink

and holds her back.

All the children laugh

and LAUGH.

There is no escape.

Scarlet is alone...

very alone...

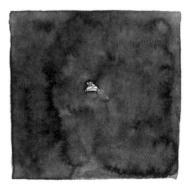

very, very alone...

Until the school bell chimes,
then Scarlet runs away...

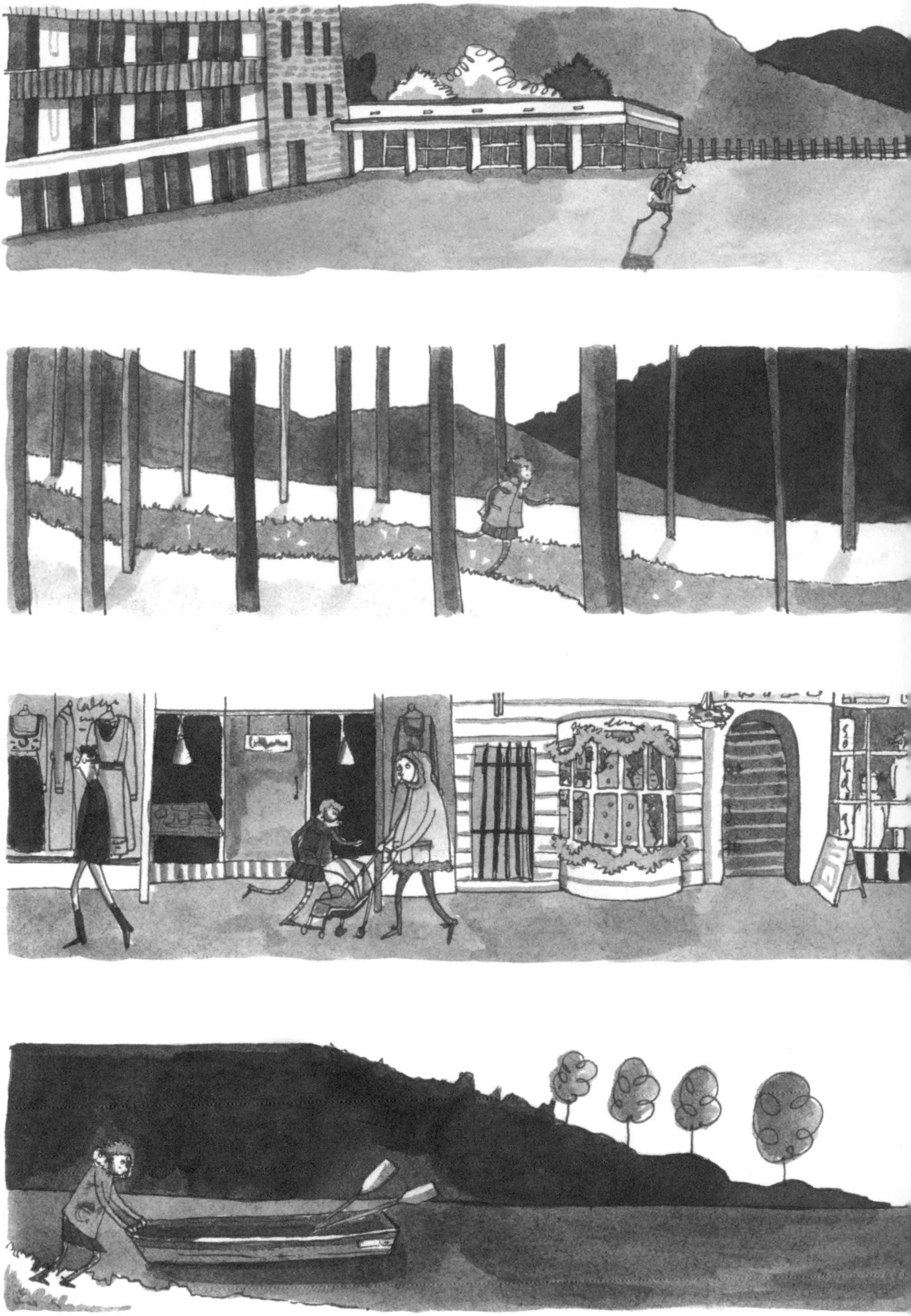

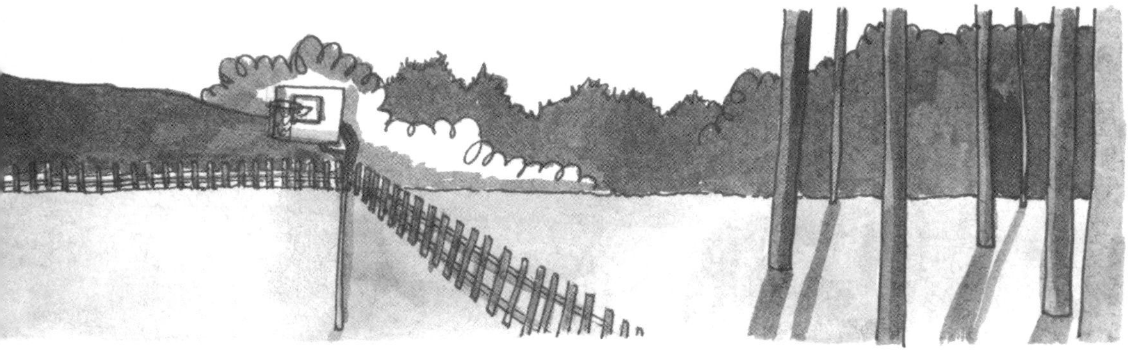

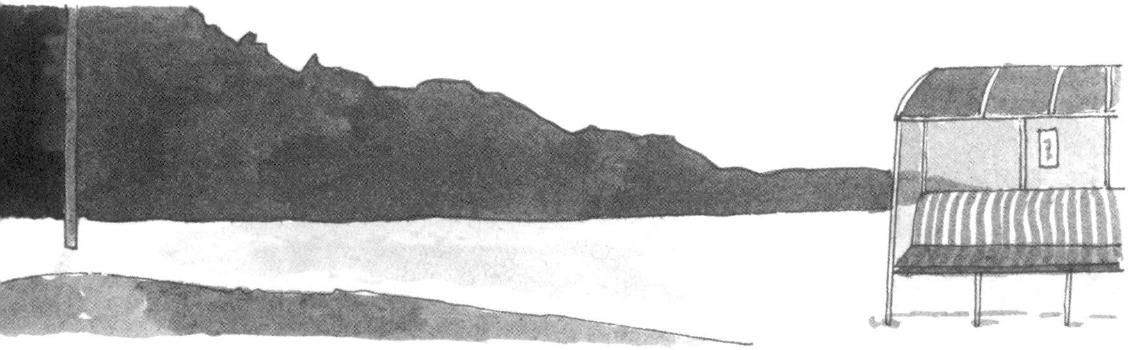

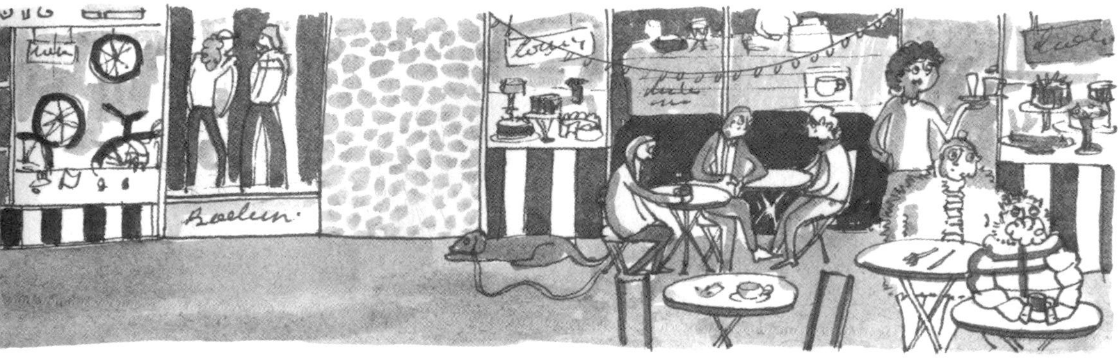

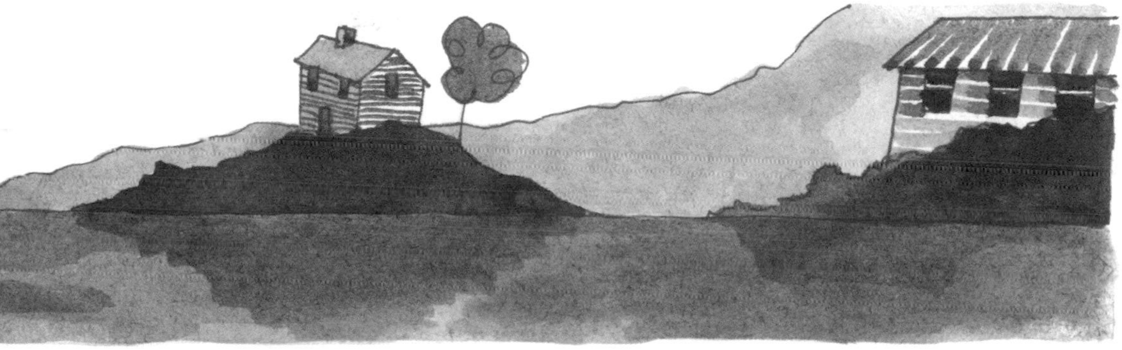

To the comfort and warmth of her Grandma's house.

And over hot chocolate

and a few marshmallows, she shares her troubles and some tears with Grandma.

Grandma listens to her problems and knows just how to help.

She opens a cupboard

and pulls out something special.

She holds it up to Scarlet and says:

'This was my mother's coat
and although it's very old,
with a zip it's now a hoodie and
it's yours to wear to school.'

Scarlet slips into the hoodie
and feels a warmth inside.

Hugged with happiness
and hope, she breaks out
into a smile.

The next day at school, now dressed in her red hoodie,

Scarlet doesn't feel the cold wind blowing through the playground any more.

Greta storms up to her

and gives Scarlet a poke,

then teases her loudly

so everyone can hear.

As the children all laugh,

Scarlet pulls on the strings that close up her hoodie – and then the strangest thing happens...

The laughter stops.
Everything goes silent,
like day has turned to night
but someone forgot to put out the Moon.
Not a sight to be seen,
not a word to be heard.
Then suddenly Scarlet hears screaming...
the noise of an angry beast?

SCARLET HOOD

Scarlet opens her hood and everywhere she sees fire.

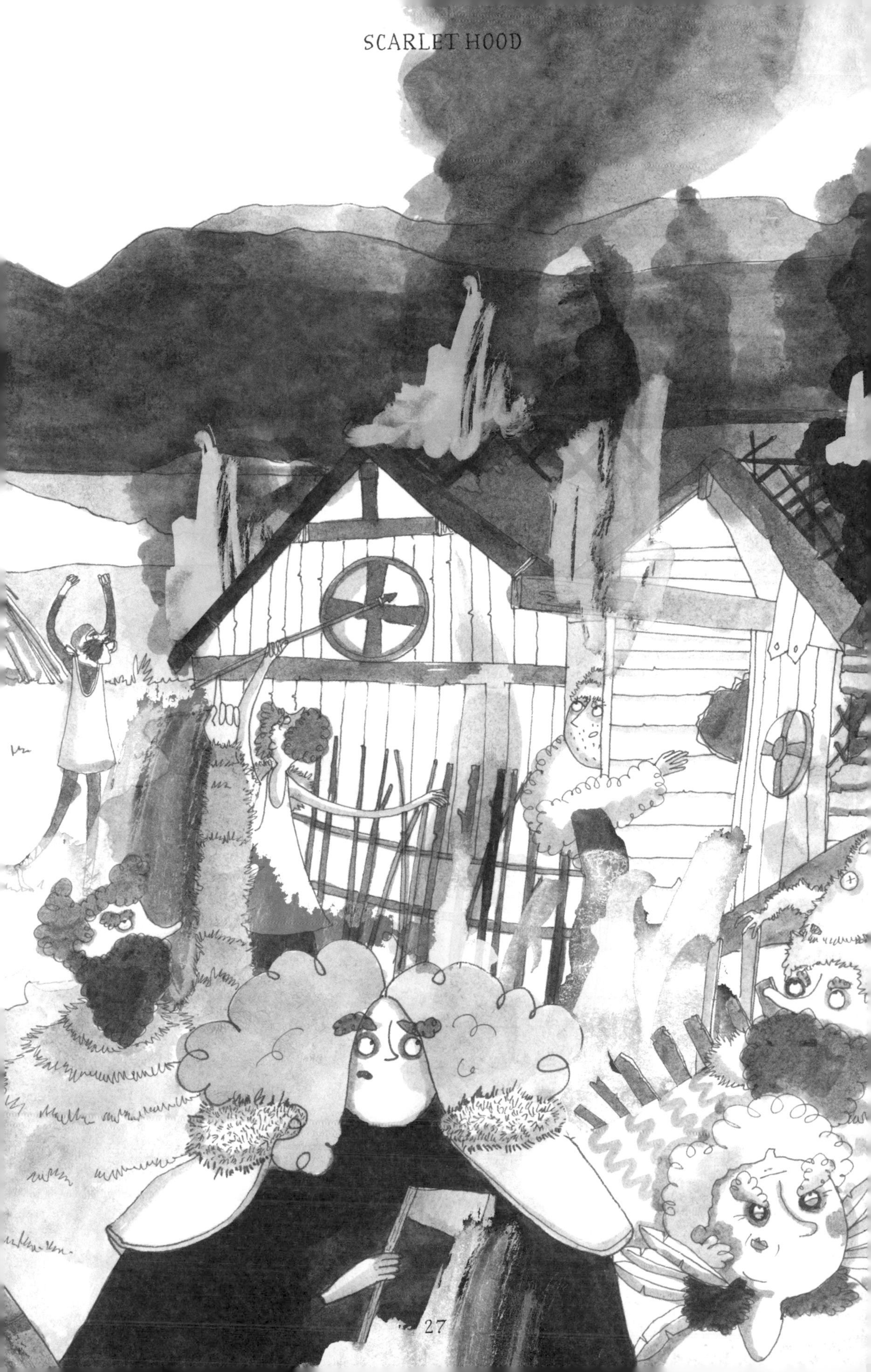

She sees strange people on the run.

The smoke blinds her vision.

Someone pulls her away

as a great flame bursts

and a loud growling sound makes the ground shake.

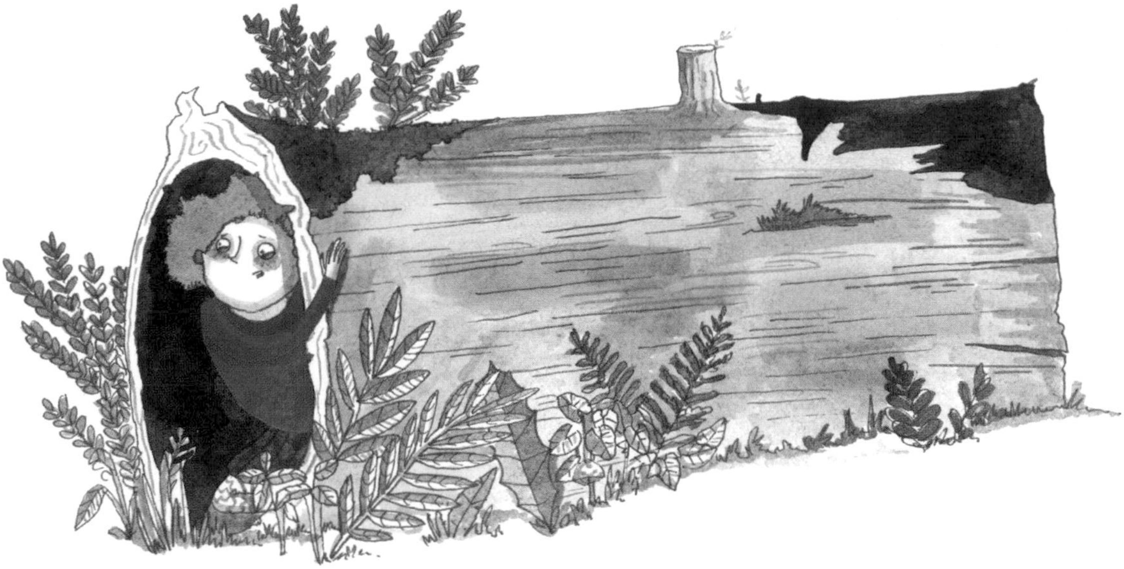

Hiding under a log, she peeks out into the smoke.

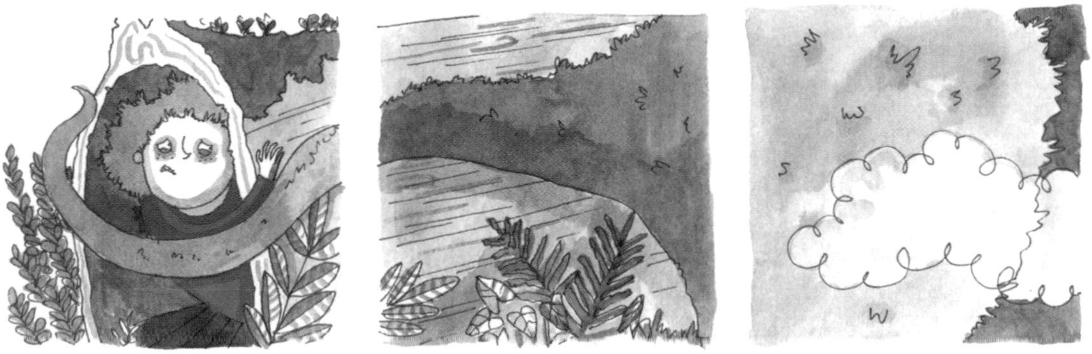

A long, furry tail trails behind thundering legs...

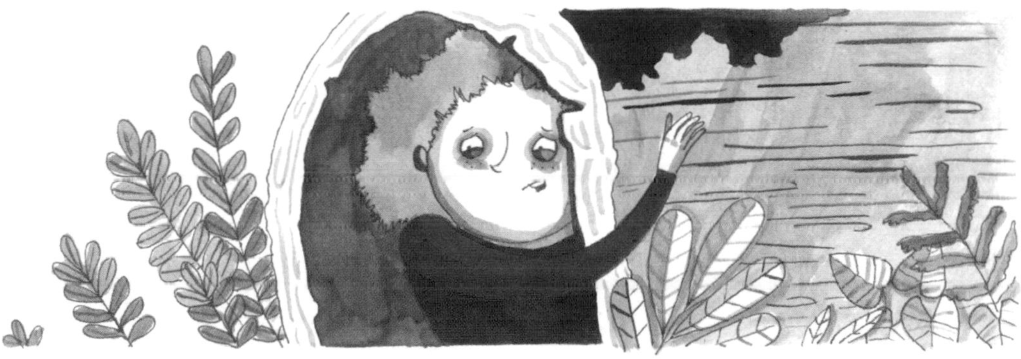

As the sound drifts off and the flames settle down,

the people all come out

from where they were hiding.

They all look like Vikings in a burnt Viking village.
Her magic red hoodie has taken her back in time!

Everyone is now staring at this strange girl.

And so the villagers take her to Katla.

Katla is a woman   who is old   and wise.

says Scarlet, alarmed.

The villagers don't listen, her protests are ignored.

I'LL BE A BARBECUE FEAST!

Katla gets her a helmet,

a sword

BUT I'M JUST A CHILD!

and a shield

and sends her up the mountain –

up icy, jagged rocks,

towards thundery skies.

She reaches a large cave.

Scarlet raises her blade, then a booming voice says...

Two angry eyes appear in the darkness.

I can read your mind.

It is racing with fright

and I see you don't wish me harm.

So I promise not to eat you.

I'm the last of my kind,

the last dragon on Earth,

and I need a place to hatch these eggs.

'And I need to find a safe place to hatch these baby dragon eggs.'

Scarlet remembers a place
where the dragon
can live in peace, and for
a thousand years no
humans will come.

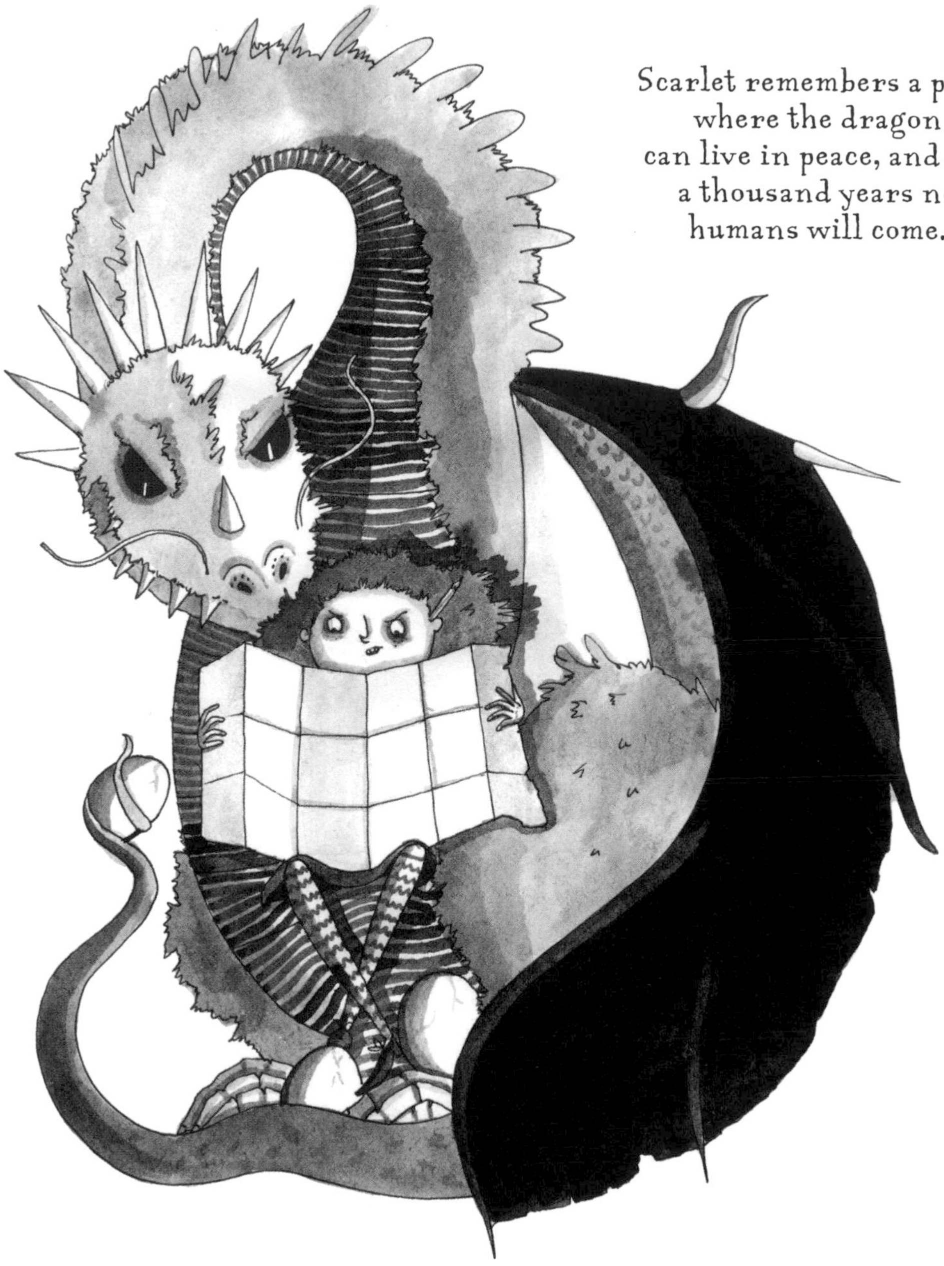

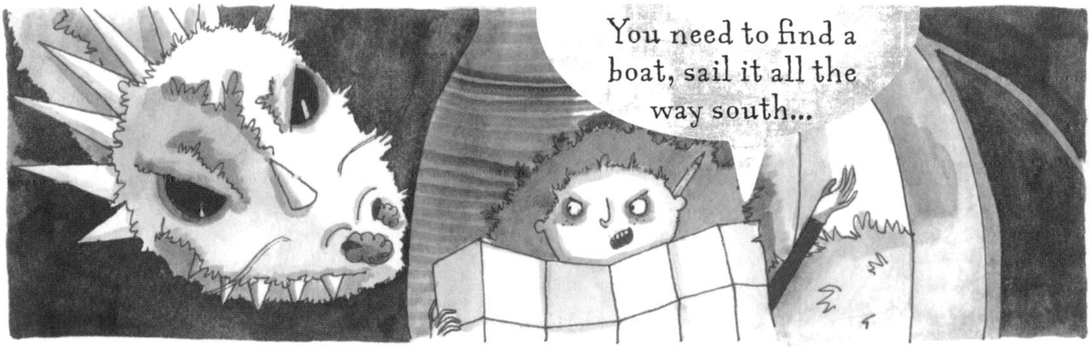
You need to find a boat, sail it all the way south...

'...and you will find a home that will offer you protection.'

So in the dark of night

they put their plan in motion,

and while the villagers sleep

they creep down to the beach.

Near moonlight-tickled waves, they find a Viking longboat.

The dragon holds out its paw,   revealing a gold tooth   which it offers to Scarlet.

There is great power to be found in a dragon's tooth. When you hold it tight you will be able to read minds.

This is yours to keep for saving my life.

Use it wisely, my friend.

SCARLET HOOD

Your kindness gives me strength.
Time to go home...

The dragon hugs Scarlet.

Close your hood like before and return to your time.

Scarlet pulls on the strings and her hood closes up.

Then she opens the hood once more and she is back at school. Just like before, Greta the Cruel is trying to make fun of Scarlet.

But this time is different:

with dragon tooth in hand,

Scarlet knows it is time to stand up to this bully.

The tooth starts to glow and Scarlet sees inside Greta's mind.

Greta is alone on her bed, crying.

Scarlet knows about
her brother –

how he takes her dolls

and pulls off the arms
and legs.

He teases her

and makes her cry.

'How do you know all that?' Greta asks.

But Scarlet hugs her tight, and in that frosty playground a new friendship begins.

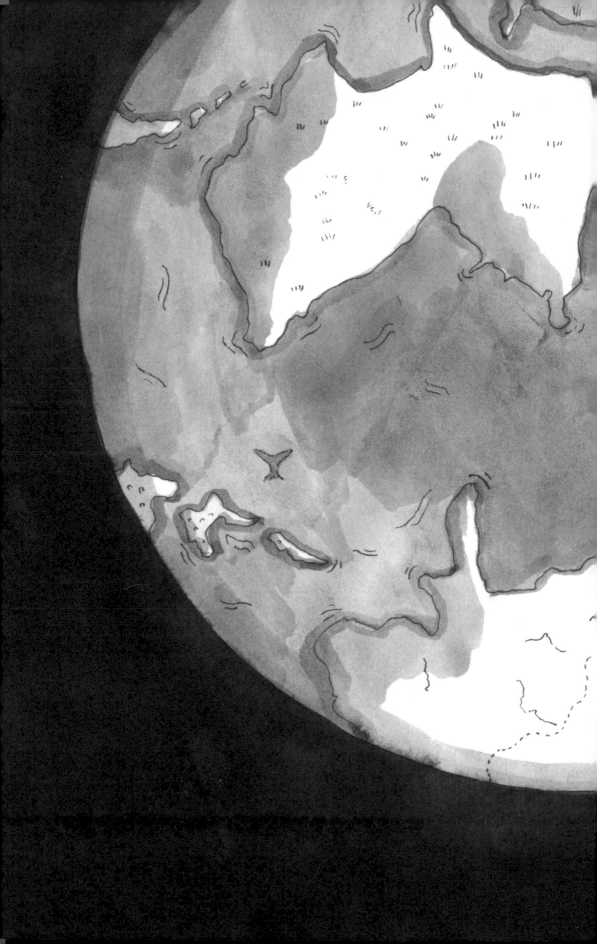

A little while later...
but also long before...
At the bottom of the world on
a white winter shore, a dragon
arrives in Antarctica.

CRACK

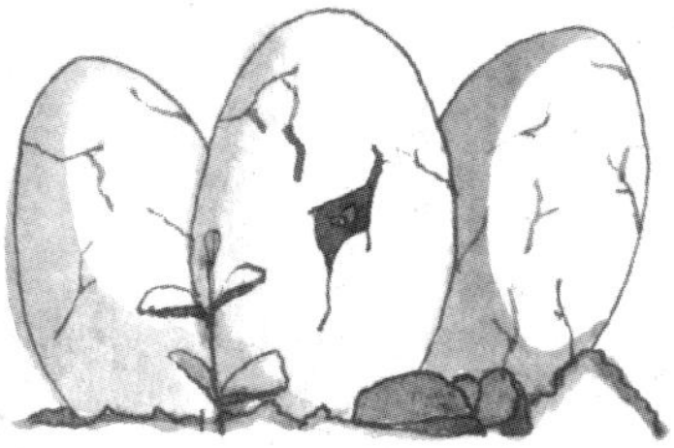

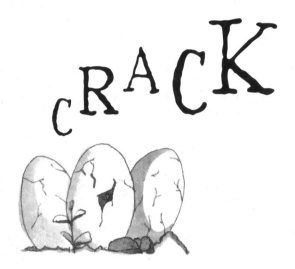